# Keeping Faith in the Dust

## by Fran Maltz

Alef Design Group

For my beloved children,
Laura, Julie, and Elliot

**LIBRARY OF CONGRESS CATALOGING-IN-PUBLICATION DATA**

Maltz, Fran, 1952–

    Keeping faith in the dust / by Fran Maltz.

       p.    cm.

    Summary: Sixteen-year-old Hannah describes the events that lead her family from their homr near the Dead Sea to the fortress at Masada, where a group of Jews hold out against the Romans for seven years.

    ISBN 1-881283-25-9 (alk. paper)

    1. Jews–History–Rebellion, 66-73–Juvenile fiction. 2. Masada Site (Israel)–Juvenile fiction.

[1. Jews–History–Rebellion, 66-73–Fiction. 2. Masada Site (Israel)–Fiction] I. Title.

    PZ7.M29847Ke    1998

    [Fic]–dc20                          98-22134

                                            CIP

                                            AC

ISBN# 1-881283-25-9

Published by Alef Design Group

ALEF DESIGN GROUP • 4423 FRUITLAND AVENUE, LOS ANGELES, CA 90058

(800) 845–0662 • (323) 582-1200 • (323) 585–0327 FAX

WWW.ALEFDESIGN.COM

MANUFACTURED IN THE UNITED STATES OF AMERICA

The Lord shall reign forever,
your God, O Zion, for all generations.
Hallelujah.
                              —PSALMS 146.10

M Y NAME IS HANNAH. I AM SIXTEEN
YEARS OLD. IN A MATTER OF HOURS
MYSELF AND ALMOST 1000 OF MY
fellow Jews, with whom I've shared this rocky
summit for the past three years, will be obliterated
from the face of this earth. I must confess though,
and may God forgive me, there were many times
when I'd tell myself that I would do anything to
stay alive—anything.

It is springtime of the year 3834*, the seventh year
of what our Roman oppressors call the Jewish
Revolt. Seven years—I can barely remember having

---

* The Hebrew year 3834 is 73 C.E.

any life before I came here. Before, I feared death; before the screaming—the killing—the running—the waiting.

And yet I did live, I am sure of it. I ran, but not in panic. I played, but not to forget the horrors of the day. I helped my parents collect olives in our grove, not boulders and arrows to hurl at our murderers.

This massive, three-tiered edifice from which I write these words soars more than 1000 feet above the Dead Sea. Once a luxurious palace built for King Herod, it is now our fortress and stronghold, but, as we have accepted with great despair, it shall not be our salvation.

I am drawn to this small, sunny nook on the upper terrace when I must be quietly alone—to think, away from the frightened voices surrounding me. Here, I scratch out these final words in hope that God, in God's infinite wisdom and mercy, will see to it that somehow our story is told; that our people shall not perish, buried under the debris of the Roman machinery of genocide. I implore my memories to become my reality. I plead for the return of the sounds of laughter and soft, light-

hearted, conversations of the past to drown out the hideous pounding echoing all around us—the ceaseless barrage of deadly rocks being catapulted against our western wall. I beg the prayers I whisper morning, afternoon, and evening each day of my life, to resound in my ears that I may no longer hear the taunting cries from the soldiers below, calling for the Jews of Masada to surrender.

For most of the day, this terrace provides refuge from the searing sun and strong south winds which plague us, and I can gaze far into the distance, upon the great expanse of what was once our homeland. The sun is very bright, and I must squint my eyes until they are nearly shut. When I do I can almost see, as I look northwards, my beloved home, Ein Gedi, a small, dry, dusty little village, close to the shores of the Dead Sea, where our olive trees grew so forgivingly in the parched, rocky soil. Their leaves, gray-green with silvery underleaf, shimmered as the breeze played in their limbs. My mother and I would sometimes pick the white, fragrant flowers which promised the fruit, and place them in our hair. This always brought an appreciative smile from my father, especially when we did so while preparing ourselves for Shabbat.

Our orchard yielded plenty of olives for us; my mother, father, and younger sister, Rebecca, had lots to sell in the market in Jerusalem, more than three days journey loaded down with our bounty, but worth every mile and blister. Jerusalem, so vast, exciting, and noisy! People crowding the streets of the lower city, selling, buying, racing here and there with pushcarts, baskets, and earthen pots of every size. And of course, our beloved Temple, whose sanctuary rising on its terraced site, was always the first image to greet me as I entered the city. Jews from all parts of the Galilee would come together here to observe and celebrate the cycle of Jewish life. Festivals in the gardens, sacrifices for the altar, and within the inner courts, discussion of important state matters. All secure behind her tall, strong walls of stone, reassuringly protected from falling as she once had, to Roman might and cruelty,

My young eyes and ears were my protection, keeping me happily unaware of the gathering darkness which was soon to take horrifying hold and eventually crush us. Frozen in that moment, Jerusalem was a cornucopia of joyous adventure. Brimming with anticipation of what the day might bring, I paid little attention to the groups of men I saw around the square huddled in urgent conversation. It was easy to ignore the merchants stockpiling weapons and food.

I accompanied my mother in the market while my father was off seeking buyers for our olives, especially abundant that year. My mother was negotiating a price for a bronze jug she wanted. The woman in the next stall was displaying items of much greater interest to a girl of thirteen. I found myself captivated by make-up palettes of vibrant reds, blues and greens, and tiny clay phials containing perfumes and delicately scented oils. She showed me a most beautiful painted wooden comb for my hair. I eyed it longingly. Amused, she scooped my thick, dark hair up into the comb, piling my ringlets at the top of my head. She showed me my reflection in a polished silver tray she kept for just such purposes. For an instant, I caught a glimpse of the promise of my womanhood. That was three years ago. I had no idea then, how fleeting and final a glimpse it would be.

During the trek home from our marketing in Jerusalem, my parents kept an uncomfortable silence, punctuated with an exchange of knowing, worried glances. The return to Ein Gedi had always been cheerful, with a laughing exchange of stories, and plans for the next visit. Today we were walking more quickly than I was used to. Our usual unhurried, contented pace became urgent, almost breathless.

I knew, as the fear began to churn deep in my stomach, that something was very wrong. Hoping desperately to be mistaken, I tried to bring some normalcy and familiarity to the moment. Wanting to sound carefree and whimsical, I asked my mother to tell me yet again, how she came upon the name of Hannah for me. Her voice, always soft and loving when she recounted the story of Hannah, now betrayed her, as she replied in a hushed, quivering voice,

"I am too tired now. We must get home quickly. Just keep walking."

KNEW THE STORY OF HANNAH WELL, OF COURSE, HAVING HEARD IT COUNTLESS TIMES. THOUGH THE LEGEND SOMEHOW INTRIGUED ME, I WAS ALWAYS A bit bothered that I was named for some-one who had to bear such unendurable sorrow.

Hannah was a widow with seven sons. Their lives were brought to misery and ruin during the reign of Syrian Emperor Antiochus, about 140 years ago. They were captured and brought before the tyrant, who ordered the boys, one by one to worship an idol. Each refused, quoting from Exodus,

"I, the Lord, am your God," and "You shall have no other Gods before Me."

One by one, they were killed. Finally, Antiochus came to the seventh boy. When he refused to worship the idol, the emperor offered him a whispered compromise. He would drop his ring on the floor. The boy had only to pick it up and bring it to him. Everyone witnessing this would assume that he had bowed down to the King, but actually the boy would not have performed any act of idolatry. The last of Hannah's sons refused, telling Antiochus:

"Woe to you. If you are so worried about your honor, how much more must I worry about the honor of God."

Before the boy was taken away to be executed, Hannah told him,

"My son, tell Abraham, your father, 'You erected one altar on which you prepared to sacrifice Isaac. I have erected seven altars.'

She then climbed to the roof and threw herself off.

My parents named me Hannah, they say, because it is their hope that I might posses her single-minded, unflinching devotion to God. For it is written,

"YOU SHALL LOVE YOUR GOD WITH ALL YOUR HEART, WITH ALL YOUR SOUL, AND WITH ALL YOUR MIND...."

Our people, the Pharisees, believe that the soul of the righteous passes, after death, to another body, and that the words of the Torah are taught from generation to generation through our forefathers.

I can't help but feel as though I am betraying them, but neither can I turn my mind from asking myself silently,

"What is more precious than the life we are given? If we choose Hannah's path, who will be left to teach the laws of Torah, and to whom shall we teach them? Must we not affirm our right to determine the paths which will shape our destiny?"

I had never confessed to them my worry that faced with Hannah's horror I might have chosen to bow down, and forced my children to do the same. Wouldn't God want us to survive, to go on at any cost? What if the last of Hannah's sons bent for the emperor's ring. Would it have been such an abomination if the witnesses merely **believed** the boy was worshipping the King?

Each time I wrestled with the story of of my name-sake, I despaired that I could not be the Hannah my parents envisioned.

Before reaching home, we stopped at the home of our neighbors, who were keeping our little Rebecca while we were in Jerusalem. They rushed out of their house to meet us, their faces as drawn with fear as my parents' faces were. Rebecca and I were shooed away to play while they spoke. A short while later we were summoned, and the four of us returned to our home, treading as quickly and silently as before.

Finally, once inside, my mother and father sat me down at our small wooden kitchen table, to try, through their tears, to explain the unexplainable. For how does one tell a child, who has known only lovingkindness, mercy and laughter, that the violence and lunacy of the world is about to come crashing down her door?

We were told to pack quickly, taking only what was essential and valuable. In the hours that followed, I knew that my time as a child had ended. My father talked late into the night about the events taking place around us—overwhelming us—a conflagration which would eventually destroy us.

"Try to understand, my small one. It is no longer safe to stay in Ein Gedi. Roman soldiers are raiding the nearby villages killing as many as they can for the mere pleasure of it, and taking children as slaves."

"But why?" I asked incredulously. "We have done nothing to them. We believe in leading a good and moral life. We take care of one another. We choose good over evil! How can this be happening to us? Why would anyone hurt us without cause? Surely, God would not let this happen, Father. If we just give God time, God will see our need, and help us. Isn't that what you have always taught us? Please don't make us leave here! This is our home!" This was all incomprehensible to me. I let the sorrow that overcame me with its crushing weight, too heavy to bear, spill out in wracking sobs, my head falling on my folded arms.

My father stroked my hair, gently brushing it away from my tear soaked, fiery cheeks. He lifted my face so that my eyes were level with his. It was easy to read his anguish and concern for the future of the family he strove so hard to protect. There was something else in his gaze as he looked at me. There was the look of steel behind his eyes.

"Shall I tell you then, Hannah, of what has been happening all around you, since before you were born? Shall you at last hear all that your mother and I hoped to spare you?" He looked to my mother, who was holding a sleepy Rebecca with one arm, while preparing a large sack of dried fruit for our departure. My mother glanced at him quickly, nodding her agreement.

Put not your trust in the great,

in mortal man who cannot save.

His breath departs;

he returns to the dust;

on that day his plans come to nothing.
—PSALMS 146.3

HIS NARRATIVE WAS A FRIGHTENING COLLAGE OF HATRED, VIOLENCE, AND CHAOS.

The Romans first occupied Judea 100 years ago, irritating us with their taxes, which became more and more punitive. Next, they began appointing our leaders, our High Priests in the Sanhedrin, the very people we had always turned to for leadership. Roman leaders demonstrated their outright contempt for the Jew by defiling the Temple with statues of Roman deities to be worshipped. They burned Torah scrolls and began sacking villages in the Gallilee. Those prominent in the Sanhedrin, convinced that fate had already determined the destiny of the Jew, were anxious to keep their positions of power and favor. They rallied citizens of Jerusalem against the growing number of those calling for the overthrow of Rome and her tyrannical, sometimes maniacal leaders.

We were dividing ourselves, sect against sect, one mistrustful of the other. Heads of government in the Sanhedrin, like High Priest Anan, desperate to keep their grip on the powerful status they had attained through the precarious favor of Rome, were calling for the death of those opposing them. They were supported by the wealthier, older population of Judea, who were in favor of capitulation to Rome. Younger, opposing rival leaders, Simon in Jerusalem, and John in the Galilee, gathered forces against the supporters of those who would accept the status quo, spreading contempt for the Sanhedrin, now believed to be a Roman puppet. What to do with one in support of the governing body? Execution. Thousands had already been killed by the hand of their brother.

With civil war and derision, the Romans had plenty of time to demonstrate their own contempt for the Jew; for his denial of idols and emperors; his adherence to strict dietary laws; his dedication to Torah; the Sabbath and a moral life. If Israel is a nation unified in its love of the law of the One God, why was that not enough to unite us against those who would use any means to depose Him? The crescendo of the din being created drowned out the howls of the wolf at the door.

The Romans patiently waited for their prey, until our own internal strife had weakened us irrevocably. It no longer mattered that some wanted to appease Rome, to find some peace in the madness, while others would refuse under penalty of death. While we enfeebled our own ranks, they began devastating the towns and countryside around Jerusalem, rooting us out, ridding the land of the leper.

That night my father taught me a new word I had never heard before—Kanaim—Zealot—one so fervent in his belief, that he will refuse to bow to the

oppressor, regardless of consequence. Oh, Hannah,
why do I feel your hand on my shoulder?

Hear, O women, the word of the Lord,
Let your ears receive the word
 of God's mouth,
And teach your daughters wailing,
And one another lamentation.
For death has climbed through
 our windows,
Has entered our fortresses,
To cut off babes from the streets,
Young men from the squares.

—JEREMIAH 9.19

A FEW DAYS BEFORE PASSOVER, TITUS, NEWLY APPOINTED HEAD OF THE JUDEAN CAMPAIGN, ALONG WITH HIS army of thousands, SET up camp just outside Jerusalem, making preparations to stamp out the very heartbeat of Judaism. Surrounded from without and within her walls, God's Chosen found themselves suffocating in a death knot of their own handiwork, as civil war and executions continued. The zealots, seizing control, executed Anan and other moderates, and threw their bodies to the dogs.

Zealot leaders from warring factions struggled for control and power, each convinced that their ideals and strategies for dealing with the Romans were the only road worth taking.

After more brutal clubbing and stabbing, much of which occurred within the inner chambers of the Temple, two contending parties emerged–those who followed John of Gischala, and those who counted themselves with Simon.

By summer of 3831, our beloved Jerusalem was a seething cauldron of murder, famine, and pestilence. The city we all believed to be impregnable, invincible, was under siege once more.

We arrived just after the heady but short-lived Judean victory over the Roman tenth legion, just outside the city. Embarrassed and enraged by the setback, Titus determined to bring to an end the Jewish uprising plaguing him for so many years.

His men constructed battering rams and catapults, marvels of engineering, from which they relentlessly pounded and hurled stones to destroy the walls protecting the city. We tried with all our might and breath to dismantle the hideous machinery, setting fire to the supports from underground, hurling firebrands at the edifices, throwing ourselves on the Roman troops, screaming, punching, tearing at flesh. My father took part in many of these passionate, frenzied raids, many of them successful, while my mother, sister and I quaked in fear, praying for his safe return.

Though we were heartened by our occasional brief victories, Titus's deadly advance, the unrelenting droves of well-disciplined, mail-clad soldiers numbering in the thousands would prove to be too much for us.

My family and I had found shelter with a distant cousin of my father, a wool merchant, whose pillaged and ransacked shop could be found with others like the smithy, the cloth maker, and the perfumery, down the winding, narrow alley of the marketplace. With aching heart I asked myself how this could be the same marketplace which only a few weeks earlier had delighted and excited my every sense? Now, looted and trampled by the Romans, it appeared a dark, twisted smile with its teeth crumbling and ripped away.

As the weeks went by, famine became our greater enemy. It was becoming more and more difficult to find fresh food. Water was becoming scarce as well. We tried to be very careful about limiting the amount of food we would eat each day. My mother gave my sister and I most of what little we had, but after a short while, even the dried berries and bits of grain were gone. Desperation had overcome many around us and they took to searching the sewers for bits of vile, repulsive matter to be coveted and fought for. For the first time in my life, I knew thirst and hunger, fear being the only taste in our mouths, day in, day out, from the moment we arose from our uneasy, troubled sleep.

Our sweet little Rebecca began to cry continually. Her once supple, energetic body had become birdlike, and her abdomen swelled frighteningly. My mother, with tears rolling down her cheeks unchecked, tried her best to soothe her, rocking her in her arms and singing familiar songs of little girls at play. Little girls who existed, it seemed, a thousand years ago.

"Why," I begged my father, "do we not surrender? Josephus, a fellow Jew, a learned historian, is pleading for us to do so. He knows the Romans well, Father. He does not see them as we do. He knows their might, their wealth. Perhaps he knows more than we do. Shouldn't we listen to him? The Romans will surely feed us if we go to them. Look at us, Father! Look at Rebecca! She is dying before our eyes! We must save ourselves no matter the cost!" Though I spoke of Rebecca, I must confess that I was in a state of panic when I thought about my own fate as well. Cupping my chin gently in his strong hand, my father turned my face toward him.

"Hannah, Hannah—You find Josephus so wise? Are you awed by the might and wealth of the Romans? Thus sayeth the Lord, my dear one,

"Let not the wise man glory in his wisdom—let not the strong man glory in his strength—Let not the rich man glory in his riches. But only in this should one glory: In his earnest devotion to Me. For I the Lord act with kindness, justice, and equity in the world; For in these I delight."

'Kindness'? 'Justice'? Where were they to be found, living in this squalor, surrounded by filth and refuse, the dying and the dead. By now the oppressive summer heat was working its evils upon us. The stench of bodies and sewage rotting in the streets created a nauseating vapor that hung over the city and seemed to cling cruelly to the lining of my nostrils. Mothers were stealing food from the mouths of their babies. Was this God's 'equity'?

Looking at my father, I noticed how prominent his cheekbones had become, how gaunt he appeared, with dark, blue-gray circles under his sunken eyes, At the same time, though, also visible in those starving eyes, was the same strength and resolve I had seen the night he unfolded his plan to come to Jerusalem—the night I learned that I was the daughter of a people struggling for survival, battling the giant for its very soul.

He went on, "If we were to turn ourselves over to the Romans, do you think they would give us food and water and send us on our way? Do you think we would be home in a few days, tending the olive grove and preparing for Shabbat?" My father questioned me calmly.

Shabbat. I had all but forgotten. The days and nights just seemed to blur together. How laughable to think of celebrating creation and the hope of peace, when each day was filled with obscene destruction and murderous conspiracy. We had once been worshippers. Now we were animals caught in the hunter's trap—writhing, shrieking, straining against the razor-like metal as it devours us slowly, eating through flesh, bone, and muscle, until finally we are spent and the fight is over.

My father went on, "Before they confined us to the mines as slave laborers, your mother and I would be paraded through the streets, shackled, in irons while the Romans look on laughing, shouting insults throwing stones, rotten food, or whatever they wish at us. While this was happening, you and your sister would be violated and beaten, then sold off into slavery. They would take from you everything that makes you human, Hannah, and every freedom you have ever known. You would no longer be a Jew. They would crush your spirit as they would a walnut."

I couldn't bear to tell him or even admit to myself that I felt as though I had no spirit left to crush.

HELD MY TONGUE AS I LISTENED TO HIS PLAN. WE WERE TO SEEK REFUGE FOR A DAY OR TWO IN THE TEMPLE. THERE WE WOULD MEET UP WITH Rabbi Jochanan ben Zaccai, who miraculously was granted permission to establish a Jewish school in Jamnia, some distance from Jerusalem. He was a pious and educated man, a Pharisee like ourselves, who believed in and preached the teachings of Rabbi Hillel. My father would ask him to take Rebecca and I as students. Still convinced the Jews would triumph, my parents would fight on with the others for the survival of the Temple. He and my mother would find us in Jamnia soon after the siege ended.

For the first time in months, I felt the stirrings of hope. My eyes filled with tears, and I became dizzy. I wanted so badly to believe that in a few days the terror would be over and we would all be starting a new life in Jamnia.

We gathered ourselves together and made our way to the Temple as night fell. Rebecca was too weak to walk, so I carried her the five miles to the upper city and our destination. So light and frail, like a rag doll in my arms. She was quiet for most of the walk, but asked softly several times,

"Hannah, are we going home now?

"Don't worry, Rebecca, soon we will be safe in our new home, and you shall have plenty to eat." I reached into the basket I was carrying, and fed her the last bits of the bread I had been rationing for myself.

As we approached the Temple, a band of men carrying torches could be seen on their way to the Roman battering rams, painstakingly constructed over a period of several weeks. At the same time John of Gischala, and his men were working underground, in tunnels they had dug under the war machines. Suddenly, with a thunderous crash, the ground under the apparatus gave way, engulfing the Roman machinery in flames. We silently cheered, gladdened by the knowledge that the Romans would rebuild their hateful weaponry with much difficulty. Their insatiable need for wood had already decimated the countryside, stripping away all the trees for a radius of ten miles around the city. Now they would have to transport their materials over a longer distance. Perhaps we had bought ourselves a little time.

This was not to be. Instead, in retaliation, Titus sealed off the city, hoping the Jews would either surrender or be starved to their death. A secret night attack on the fortress of Antonia, formerly a stronghold for John of Gischala, drove the Jewish sentinels into the Temple. The battle was now at our very gates. Hundreds of Jews, using all their strength and courage, succeeded in repelling the Romans in a hand-to-hand brutal battle of tremendous fury.

Each instance of Jewish triumph against Rome fueled Titus' fervor to bring the Temple, the core of Jewish strength, to ruin. Frustrated attempts to destroy the Northern Gate, battering rams and catapults reduced to rubble, soldiers killed by bands of starving zealots—victories all—which in the end would condemn us to our inescapable demise.

The vivid memory of our final moments in the Temple has all but devoured me, It tears at my very being, leaving my soul in jagged shards.

Titus at last issued the order to set the Temple gates on fire. After burning for an entire day, he ordered that the fires be extinguished to allow for the advance of his legions. Overcoming their fatigue and fear, the defenders of the Temple fought on against the Romans at the gates. Despite our passion, we found ourselves cornered, with the enemy pursuing us to the Sanctuary itself.

Panic-stricken and hysterical, thousands fled to one of the porticos in the outer court. From there we watched in horror as flames shot up from the chambers surrounding the Sanctuary. A chilling chorus of desperation and despair rose up from terrified women and children wailing and screaming for husbands, fathers, brothers, and sons they would never see again. Through my own tears, I whispered urgent prayers for the safety of my father,

pleading with God to let him find us and save us. The blaze darkened the sky and filled the air with heavy, acrid smoke.

Shrieking and howling crescendoed as the Romans, intoxicated now by their murderous frenzy, and having wreaked their merciless havoc in the Sanctuary, charged toward the portico, slaying all in their path.

The smoke and mayhem made thinking, for that matter seeing, all but impossible. I picked up Rebecca and grabbed my mother's outstretched arm. Hoping to find my father, we began running, my sister clinging to me with all of the strength she had left in her starved, frail body; three terrified victims in a throng of thousands madly fleeing in different directions.

It was crucial that the three of us stay together. We must not lose sight of each other. People fell all around us; choking on the smoke, run through by Roman swords, trampled by the horde. We pushed on, our eyes frantically searching the mob for my father; shoving, side-stepping, climbing over piles of bodies. No time to stop, to look down, to mourn.

Make our way to the Sanctuary. Find my father. This was our only mission.

I didn't see the Roman soldier who killed my sister. I had turned my head for a moment to locate my mother in the mob when I felt the force of his sword as he lunged at us.

Hearing Rebecca scream, I looked down to see her tiny ashen face twisted with pain. I held her closer to me, as her warm blood soaked through my clothes. All at once my legs felt leaden. I couldn't breathe. It was as if all the air had been sucked from the universe. Run faster, I commanded myself. Don't let mother see. If mother doesn't know, then it hasn't happened. Find father. Everything will be alright. Think clearly! What is your name? My name is Hannah. Where are you? I am in Jerusalem. What day is today? Today is the ninth of Ab—the anniversary of the Roman destruction of the first Temple—the day the Romans burned the second Temple, our Temple—the day I lost my sister.

Somehow, at last, I made my way to the Sanctuary, only to find it charred and looted. The Romans had confiscated, among other treasures, our Torah scrolls and beautiful Menorah, intending to display them as cruel spoils in their victory celebration. Searching for my father, my eyes desperately scanned the small group of dazed men milling about, mumbling half-hearted plans for retribution.

He saw us first, and hurried to embrace us with arms open wide, his weary face glowing with joy and relief. My mother rushed in behind me and reached for him. It wasn't until he was within inches of us that he realized, as he looked at her lifeless body cradled in my arms, that Rebecca was dead. The color drained from his cheeks as he cried out in a chilling voice I had never heard before,

"Rebecca! Rebecca! My God! What has happened to you?!"He took my sister from me and sank to his knees, crushing her to his chest, Holding her delicate face in his hands, he covered her lifeless features with tender, sobbing kisses, as my mother, faint with shock, fell in a heap next to him. Their soul-wrenching wails were more than I could bear. Not a day has passed that I do not hear their echo. The three of us huddled over our little Rebecca, stoking her hair, crying out her name, kissing her

our final good-byes. As we wept, we knew that there would be no end to our mourning.

My parents gently laid Rebecca on the altar, where she would rest with the scores of bodies already piled hundreds deep. There they lay, a bizarre, and horrifying sacrifice to a heedless God. The encircling fires crept closer, and would soon engulf the innocent offerings. Finally, we tore ourselves from her side, and along with a few remaining, stupefied survivors, left the Sanctuary. Under cover of darkness, with hearts black and heavy, we left behind forever, our sacred Temple, beloved Jerusalem, and cherished Rebecca.

The Romans had set fire to the entire city. They began the inferno in the lower city, then ignited and gutted the upper city, massacring all who remained in their path. Thorough to the end, they were sure to root out any who sought shelter within their homes or hid in the sewers.

Where were our steadfast leaders now; those ambitious men who waged such a ferocious and foolish battle against each other? Men who had no understanding of words like tolerance, unity, brotherhood—Simon and John requested Titus' permission to take to the desert with their families, leaving Jerusalem to the Roman victors. Infuriated, Titus responded by razing what was left of the city.

Oh, Israel! Now you are but ashes—an unrecognizable sacrifice **you** delivered to the altar.

For the sake of Zion I will not be silent,
For the sake of Jerusalem I will not be still,
Till her victory emerge resplendent
And her triumph like a flaming torch.
Nations shall see your victory,
And every king your majesty;
And you shall be called by a new name
Which the Lord Himself shall bestow.
You shall be a glorious crown
In the hand of the Lord—
                              —ISAIAH 62

AFTER TRAVELING SOUTH ON FOOT FOR DAYS, WE ARRIVED AT THE FOOT OF MASADA, EXHAUSTED AND DRAINED OF emotion. THE treacherous, three and a half mile climb to this last outpost of Jewish survival seemed more than we could muster. We were unable to remember when we had last had anything to eat or drink. Our depleted bodies and souls were numb with weariness and despair.

Knowing no other choice, we began our ascent, careful to keep our footing on the dangerously narrow, twisting path, ever mindful of the threatening, jutting cliffs and ravines on either side. At the end of our arduous four hour hike, we found ourselves standing shakily atop the plateau fortress known as Masada. We gratefully filled our lungs with deep breaths of the clean, clear air, and gladly let the warm desert wind whip our hair about our faces. Though our muscles trembled with fatigue and uncertainty, we took comfort, as we surveyed the faces welcoming us, that the ground beneath our feet was sound, and the people with whom we stood, resolute.

I was struck by the irony of this tiny band of Jews seeking shelter and survival on this rocky peak. Less than one hundred years ago King Herod fashioned and fortified Masada as a vacation palace; a luxurious refuge from the daily trials of leadership. Still more ironic, is that one of the most troublesome woes from which he fled, was his growing discord with the Jews and his fear that they would depose him. I couldn't decide if the long dead King would be angry at these irksome Jews for trespassing on the splendor he had so carefully created, or be laughing at us for allowing ourselves to come to such a desperate and miserable end.

We were greeted by Leib, his wife Leah, and their eight year old daughter Kerith, residents here since the beginning of the rebellion, in 3827. We were led to the lower of the three terraces, and shown to what would be our living quarters.

The large, earthen walled chamber was a welcome sight to me. Ours was a 14 yard long subdivision of what was once a larger dwelling. Our hosts had been hastily dividing the larger chambers to accommodate families such as ours; refugees of the terror of the Roman world below. The wall cupboards were generously filled for us with vegetables, grains, walnuts, dates, olives, clay pots, bronze pans, and wooden cooking utensils.

While Leah helped my mother prepare bread in the mud oven, I fell upon my soft straw bed and slept without stirring, for what seemed like days. My first thoughts as I woke in the quiet, dimly lit room, were of Rebecca. My eyes instinctively sought her out. I knew that like me, she would want to explore our strange and wondrous new home. I reminded my eyes, with renewed sadness, that the search was futile.

With Kerith as my guide, I investigated the mysteries of Masada for days, delving into each nook and crevice. Together we enjoyed the bath houses, delighting in the water warmed by clay pipes beneath the floor. There was also a refreshing cool water pool, and most importantly, to our adult community, the Mikves. The Jews of Masada had taken great pains to construct two ritual baths, engineering the structures so that plaster conduits collected rain water, then channeled it into the baths, purifying it.

Playing sentry, we would climb Herod's many protective towers and dutifully scour the sun-drenched Judean wilderness for an imaginary approaching Roman army. Countless hours were spent inspecting the ornate splendors of Herod's former palaces and hanging villas; wall paintings, intricately designed, multi-clolored mosaic floors, majestic columns engraved with scrollwork, private hot and cold baths, and vast living quarters.

Herod the Great! What would you think now of your beautiful mosaic floors, covered with our ovens and soot? How your heart would break to witness your walls and pillars, carved with meticulous artistry, ripped apart and re-used by my people. You would weep to learn that your exquisite wall paintings have been hidden by our hastily constructed bath houses, bakeries and dwellings.

Unlike you, powerful Emperor, we have neither time nor use for the luxuries you fashioned here. **Our Masada is rich with the hope of survival.**

Kerith proved to be a good friend, listening quietly when I spoke of Rebecca and the holocaust of Jerusalem. The two of us talked for hours about our homes, and even wept together for a way of life we knew would never be ours again.

I am forever thankful to God for the one sweet reminder of home—the gardens at the summit of

Masada. This was my favorite place to spend time. I marveled at the way the earth burst forth with new life after a downpour. Our thirsty soil would suddenly sprout waves of brightly colored flowers, and blossoms suddenly revealed their fruit.

It was fulfilling for me to tend the gardens alongside the others, knowing the only food we would eat was the food we grew. We worked well together, sharing information and techniques. I taught several of the children about olive growing, and learned for the first time about caring for pomegranate bushes and corn.

**A**S THE DAYS PASSED, I LOOKED WITH GROWING AFFECTION AND PRIDE UPON THIS HARD-WORKING, DEEPLY COMMITTED community. We had all suffered wounding loss, and were well acquainted with the fear of death. Yet, we took our strength from one another, and forged a life for ourselves filled with communal spirit, fellowship, and unfailing devotion to God.

We worshipped daily in the synagogue we fashioned for ourselves from the one Herod left behind. Miraculously, we even had Torah scrolls, and several of us spent many sweltering afternoons in the cool serenity of our Temple, studying and discussing the holy books.

As my father and I sat side by side on the cold stone benches in the stillness shortly before one of the Torah readings, I questioned aloud for the first time, the death of my sister.

"Father, why was Rebecca taken from us as she was? Wasn't God watching? How could he do this to us, knowing the grief and misery we would feel? How could he take her life like that? She was only six!"

"Hannah—" he sighed heavily. "Of course God watches. God gave us the gift of her life for six years. Does she not live forever in your heart and mind? In the things you see and do? Why do we assume, as we live our life, that we have some official claim on it, that we have a right to be here. I think I have been guilty of this myself. Sadly, it often takes a great loss, like the death of our Rebecca, to make us realize that we are here at God's pleasure; part of God's divine plan. Use your time on this earth wisely, my dear one. Look for the good around you; be grateful for God's miracles, even the smallest. "

He looked intently into my eyes, and whispered urgently,

"Never let go of your faith, Hannah. Don't ever allow yourself to become one of the disillusioned, embittered lost souls led by Moses through the wilderness following the exodus from Egypt. They were denied entry into the Promised Land, Hannah, because they lost faith. Though God's hand provided for them and protected them on their journey, they refused to see. They became weak-spirited and ungrateful.

"Our own people forgot this tragedy when they fought each other to the death for power and control in Jerusalem. Though they called themselves righteous Jews, they too had destroyed their faith, serving themselves and not the Lord. They doomed themselves to fail, Hannah, when they lost sight of their true mission: to keep faith with the Lord at all times." My father's eyes shone with a conviction that welled up from deep in his soul.

WAS WORKING IN THE GARDENS, ENJOYING THE SHORT-LIVED COOL OF MORNING. IT HAD RAINED HEAVILY THE NIGHT BEFORE, AND THERE WAS much weeding to be done. Suddenly, Kerith came up behind me and grabbed my shoulder.

"Hannah! I saw them! They're here! Oh, God, Hannah! I am so frightened!" she cried excitedly.

"Who is here? Kerith, calm down. Who did you see?" I asked, turning to see her terrified face.

"The Roman army, Hannah. They're setting up camp at the foot of Masada! What shall we do?" She began to whimper.

I was quiet for a moment. Then, holding my dear friend in my arms, I told her firmly, "We shall fight them. And we shall never surrender!"

I dropped my tools and taking Kerith by her trembling hand, set out to find my father.

We had prepared for this inevitable siege by carefully storing and rationing our food and water over the years. We used our own coins, struck here at Masada to purchase food and goods. I thought our coins were very beautiful. The ones I most admired were bronze and bore a vine-leaf design on one side and a chalice on the other.

The inscription read: "For the Freedom of Zion." Others marked the years of revolt.

Our storehouses were kept full of grains, vegetables, and other staples. The water in the vast cisterns, ingeniously designed by Herod's engineers, would quench our thirst for years to come.

The former Emperor had also unwittingly provided us with the beginnings of an arsenal, and we spent much time crafting our own bows and arrows, spears and swords. During the past several months, we had been busily collecting large rocks to be honed and heaved at our attackers whenever they might arrive. With little else left to do, we began keeping a close eye on the activities of the enemy below.

Day after day the vigil continued, as we watched Silva set up his garrisons at strategic points. He had the Jewish prisoners he brought with him construct a wall around Masada to close off possible routes of escape, and posted sentinels to guard these positions.

Our only comfort was knowing that food and water for the General and his men had to be brought in from afar, while we enjoyed both at our fingertips.

With his wall completed, Silva's strategy for our annihilation became clear. He chose the west face of the fortress to construct an earthen embankment, raised some three hundred feet. On top of this, he had built a platform of great stones fitted closely together. It was obvious that this was to be the mount for his war engines.

As the work continued, the mood among my fellow Zealots grew somber and anxious. My mother and the other women worked very hard at occupying themselves with routine tasks. They gardened, cooked, and tended the children, their faces tight with fear. I began to miss the comfort of my mother's usual lively conversation, as the growing terror settled upon us, bringing a silence that was deafening.

AWOKE EARLIER THAN USUAL ONE GRAY MORNING AND RAN TO THE BATTLEMENTS TO SEE WHAT HAD BEEN ACCOMPLISHED WHILE I SLEPT. MY SLEEPY eyes flew open, and a thunderous shudder shook my entire body. The battering rams, stone-throwers, and quick-firers were in place. I gazed in horror, reliving the grisly final moments of the Armageddon that was Jerusalem.

Gazing down at the hellish instruments of death, my mind was flooded with images Rebecca. I missed her so! I could see us playing hide and seek; her mischievous little face poking out from behind the tree she thought I'd never check. There she was again, grinning with delight and triumph, wearing my leather sandals, tripping over herself, her feet dragging on the dusty earthen kitchen floor. I struggled to shut out the vision of running, carrying her starved, lifeless body, but suddenly my arms felt leaden from the weight.

As I gazed down and heard her murderers calling for our surrender, their death-trap poised and ready, I promised my little sister that I would fight them with every breath God gave me. I swore to myself that I would **never** abandon Masada.

Without warning, their catapults fired, and the first spiked stone missile was hurled at the wall which guarded the entire summit. It shrieked as it flew through the air, and crashed against our first line of defense with an impact I could feel under my feet. We ran for cover as the barrage continued, unrelenting. At the same time, the battering rams began pounding the wall in obscene concert with the stone throwers.

Jolted, we threw ourselves into full mobilization, heaving hundred pound boulders and boiling oil off the battlements; shooting steel tipped arrows at Silva's men, hoping to weaken the resolve of this determined tenth legion. Our efforts brought little harm to them and did nothing to diminish their zeal.

MUST WRITE HASTILY NOW, FOR I SENSE THAT WE ARE QUICKLY RUNNING OUT OF TIME. IT HAS TAKEN HIM SEVERAL DAYS, BUT THIS AFTERNOON, Silva succeeded in bringing down the wall we fought so hard to defend. Unbeknownst to him, we had speedily constructed another wall, behind this one. It was made from great wooden beams laid lengthwise and end to end, in two parallel rows, a wall's breadth apart. The space between was filled with earth. We were convinced that this design would withstand Silva's attack, as the blows of the engines would now fall upon yielding material. In fact the continued ramming did almost no damage.

After several frustrating barrages, Silva noticed that the inner wall was made mostly of wood. As dusk fell, he ordered his soldiers to destroy the wall

by setting it on fire. It took but a few well aimed flaming missiles to start the blaze. We watched in anguish as it began to burn. Many began to weep, knowing that by morning we would be overrun.

The flames were beginning to light up the darkening sky, when, as if God himself had exhaled a great breath, a north wind blew back the flames, driving them against the Romans. Our hearts leapt from our chests with the hope that this would reduce the Roman machinery to rubble.

Suddenly, and just as shockingly, the Lord, our God reconsidered, and finding his people Israel undeserving of deliverance after all, blew the flames back in our faces. By full dark, all that remained of our defense and our hope was a mound of smoldering ashes.

Eleazar Ben Ya'ir, the brave and wise man who was our shepherd, called together his closest men, my father among them, and spoke his final address,

"Long ago, my brave men, we resolved neither to serve the Romans, nor any other except our God. For God alone is man's true and righteous Lord.

Now the time has come when we must test our resolution by our actions. At this crisis, let us not disgrace ourselves. We refused to submit to a slavery even when it meant no physical danger to us. Let us not now accept slavery, with all of the punishments awaiting if we fall alive into Roman hands. For as we were the first of all to revolt, so are we the last in arms against them. Moreover, I believe that it is God who has granted us this favor, that we have it in our power to die nobly and in freedom, a privilege denied to others who were met with unexpected defeat.

"Our fate at break of day is certain capture. But there is still the free choice of a noble death in the company of those we hold most dear. Our enemies cannot prevent this even though they fervently hope to take us alive. Nor can we hope to defeat them in battle. Maybe, indeed, from the very first—when we chose to defend our liberty—we ought perhaps to have read God's purpose and to have recognized that the Jewish people, once beloved by Him, had been sentenced to extinction. For had God continued to be gracious, or even just a little angry, God would never have permitted such widespread destruction or have abandoned God's most Holy City to be burned to the ground by our enemies. But did we, in truth, really hope that we alone of all the Jewish nation would survive and preserve our freedom? Mark now how God exposes the vanity of our hopes. Not even the impregnable nature of this fortress has been enough to save us. Nay, though we have ample food, stores of arms, plenty for every other need, yet we have been deprived, manifestly by God Himself, of all hope of surviving. For it was not of their own accord that those flames which were driving against the enemy turned back upon the wall which we built, No, all this betokens God's wrath.

"But let us not pay the penalty for our sins to our bitterest foes, but rather to God Himself, through an act of our own hands. Let our wives die undishonored, our children with no knowledge of slavery. And when they are gone, let us render ungrudging service to each other, using our liberty as a noble winding sheet. But first let us destroy our possessions and the whole fortress by fire, for the

Romans will be deeply chagrined to find neither our persons nor anything of value to loot. Let us spare only our food supply, for it will testify, when we are dead, that it was not want which subdued us, but that as we resolved at the beginning of the war, we chose death not slavery."

"—Pity the young, whose vigorous bodies can sustain prolonged tortures, pity the more advanced in years too weak to bear such calamities. Is a man to see his wife led off to violation, to hear the voice of his child crying, 'Father,' when his own hands are bound? No! While those hands are free and can hold a sword, let us die as free men with our children and wives. Let us quit this life together!"

My father, having recounted Eleazar's impassioned plea to my mother and I in the stillness of our chamber, took us in his arms, weeping as if his heart would break.

"We have so little time left, my darlings. At this moment some of the storehouses are being burned and many of our neighbors are already dispatching their loved ones."

I AM NOT AFRAID TO DIE, BUT AM INSTEAD OVER-COME WITH AN UNBEARABLE SENSE OF MOURNING WHEN I REALIZE THAT I SHALL NOT WAKE tomorrow. I shall not have another day to tend the gardens, feel the desert sun and wind on my cheeks, or see Rebecca's face in my mind's eye. How I shall miss hours spent sitting by my father in the sanctuary, with his strong, comforting hand on mine—and hearing my mother's gentle voice and the softness of her nurturing touch.

After holding each other in silence for some time, I whispered, careful not to shatter the bliss of our final moments together,

"Eleazar is wise in all he has said, but for one thing: God does **not** mean for God's people Israel to become extinct. Like Moses' flock, we are simply not ready to be a free people. I have no fear. Somehow we shall endure. Remember the students of Rabbi Yochanan, just outside these borders? Certainly there must be more Jews out there, somewhere, dedicated, as we are, to serving God. Remember our coin on which was engraved, 'For The Freedom of Zion'? Generations from now, that freedom shall be ours."

As my parents set fire to our belongings, lest they be claimed by the Romans, I hurriedly scribble my final thoughts, and bury this tablet behind loose stones in the wall where it was written.

On this, the first night of Pesah, we depart from ritual. Instead of asking the angel of death to pass over our houses, we welcome him into our homes. Moses's people set forth from Egypt on their quest for freedom—we depart from Masada.

As my father draws his sword, we embrace once more, our eyes brimming with tearful farewell.

Hannah, for so long I have felt your hand on my shoulder. Tonight you open your arms and embrace me. I shall die, as you have—as our Rebecca has—as

the faithful of Masada have—*"al kiddush ha-Shem"*—
to sanctify God's name!

"No longer shall you need the sun
For light by day,
Nor the shining of the moon
For radiance by night
For the Lord shall be your light everlasting
Your God shall be your glory.
Your sun shall set no more,
Your moon no more withdraw;
For the Lord shall be a light to you forever,
And your days of mourning shall be ended.
And your people, all of them righteous,
Shall possess the land for all time—"
—ISAIAH 60.19